THE ROAD TO SANTIAGO

BY D. H. FIGUEREDO

ILLUSTRATED BY
PABLO TORRECILLA

LEE & LOW BOOKS INC.
NEW YORK

abuela (ah-BWEH-lah): grandmother

buñuelo (BOON-nyu-el-loh): fried pastry dipped in sweet syrup

Noche Buena or **Nochebuena** (NOH-chay-bwen-na): night before Christmas

Feliz Navidad (feh-LEES NAH-vi-dahd): Merry Christmas

la misa del gallo (lah mee-sah del GAH-yo): midnight mass (literally "the rooster's mass")

manigua (mah-nee-GWA): dense foliage, woods (used only in the Caribbean)

rebeldes (reh-BEHL-des): rebels

sidra (SEE-drah): Spanish cider

silencio (SEE-len-see-oh): silence

turrón (two-ROHN) / **turrones** (two-ROH-nes): nougat candy from Spain

villancicos (vi-YAHN-see-COHS): Christmas carols

Text copyright © 2003 by D.H. Figueredo
Illustrations copyright © 2003 by Pablo Torrecilla

Lee & Low Books Inc., 95 Madison Avenue, New York, NY 10016
leeandlow.com

Manufactured in China

Book Design by Christy Hale
Book Production by The Kids at Our House

The text is set in Zapf Humanist Bold
The illustrations are rendered in acrylic

10   9   8   7   6   5   4   3   2   1
First Edition

Library of Congress Cataloging-in-Publication Data
Figueredo, D. H.
The road to Santiago / by D.H. Figueredo ; illustrated by Pablo Torrecilla.— 1st ed.
p. cm.
Summary: A young boy and his family, living in Cuba in the 1950s, try their best
not to let the rebel soldiers keep them from celebrating Christmas with their
relatives in Santiago. Based on a true incident in the life of the author.
ISBN 1-58430-059-0
[1. Cuba—History—1933–1959—Fiction. 2. Christmas—Fiction.] I. Torrecilla, Pablo, ill. II. Title.
PZ7.F488 Ro 2003
[E]—dc21   2002030165

To my three muses: my wife, Yvonne,
my son, Daniel, my daughter, Gabriela;
and in memory of my father, Danilo—D.H.F.

To Barbara with all my love—P.T.

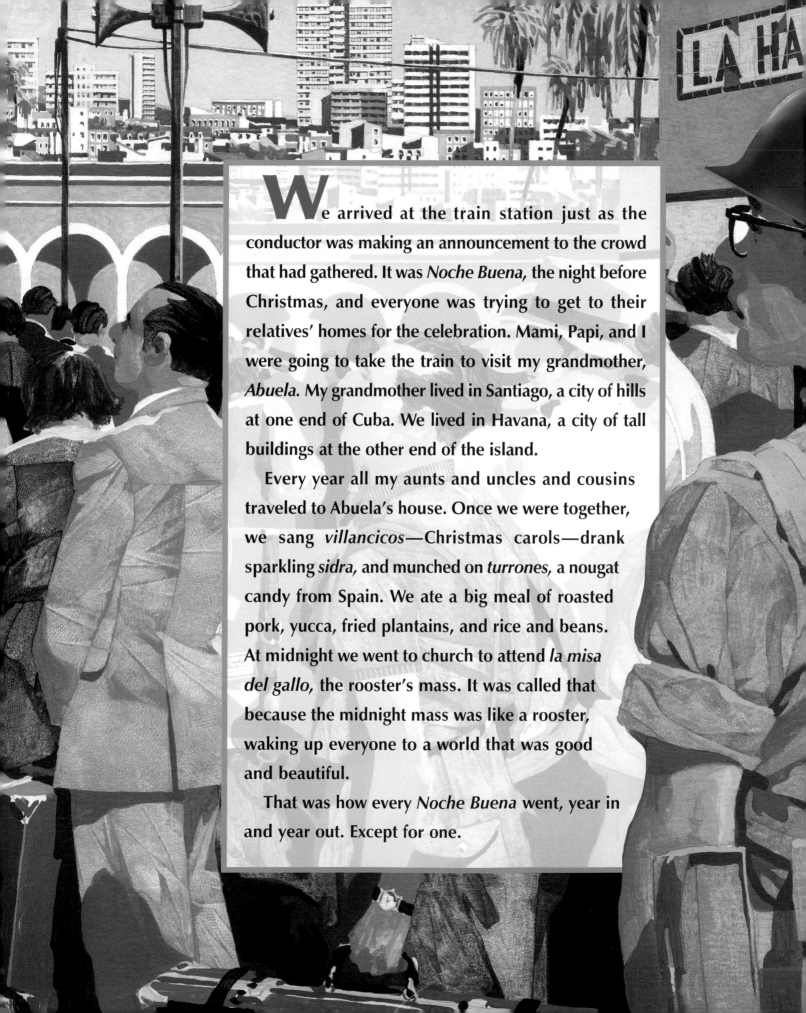

We arrived at the train station just as the conductor was making an announcement to the crowd that had gathered. It was *Noche Buena*, the night before Christmas, and everyone was trying to get to their relatives' homes for the celebration. Mami, Papi, and I were going to take the train to visit my grandmother, *Abuela*. My grandmother lived in Santiago, a city of hills at one end of Cuba. We lived in Havana, a city of tall buildings at the other end of the island.

Every year all my aunts and uncles and cousins traveled to Abuela's house. Once we were together, we sang *villancicos*—Christmas carols—drank sparkling *sidra*, and munched on *turrones*, a nougat candy from Spain. We ate a big meal of roasted pork, yucca, fried plantains, and rice and beans. At midnight we went to church to attend *la misa del gallo*, the rooster's mass. It was called that because the midnight mass was like a rooster, waking up everyone to a world that was good and beautiful.

That was how every *Noche Buena* went, year in and year out. Except for one.

That was the year war broke out. The people who were against the president formed an army and hid in the mountains. The president called them *rebeldes*—rebels—and on the day before *Noche Buena* he sent his soldiers to fight them. To stop the soldiers, the *rebeldes* blew up the railroad tracks.

When we found out the train could not go to Santiago, I was very upset. I was looking forward to playing with my cousins and eating all the tasty dishes Abuela prepared, especially a pastry she made only on *Noche Buena* called a *buñuelo*. It was shaped like the number eight, and she served it hot and dripping with honey.

As soon as we heard the news, Papi set out to find a way to Santiago. The local bus was already full, so Papi figured we needed to go to another town to catch a bus. He talked to the station manager, who told him about a farmer down the street who had a car.

Soon Papi arrived with the farmer and his car. It was long and flat and square, like the cars in old movies.

"Alfredito, this is Señor Gasparo," Papi said to me. "He's going to help us."

We put our suitcases in the trunk, but Mami held onto the bag with gifts for our relatives. There were boxes of *turrones* for Abuela and two bottles of Sidra El Gaitero, Papi's favorite drink.

We drove along a bumpy road that went through a sugar cane field. As we reached the highway, the field yielded to a patch of thick green woods, called a *manigua*.

Suddenly we heard a loud noise, and the car shook. Señor Gasparo pulled to the side of the road and jumped out.

"We have a flat tire," he declared. "I have a spare, but I don't have a jack to raise the car."

My heart sank. First the train, now the car. It seemed as if we would never get to Santiago.

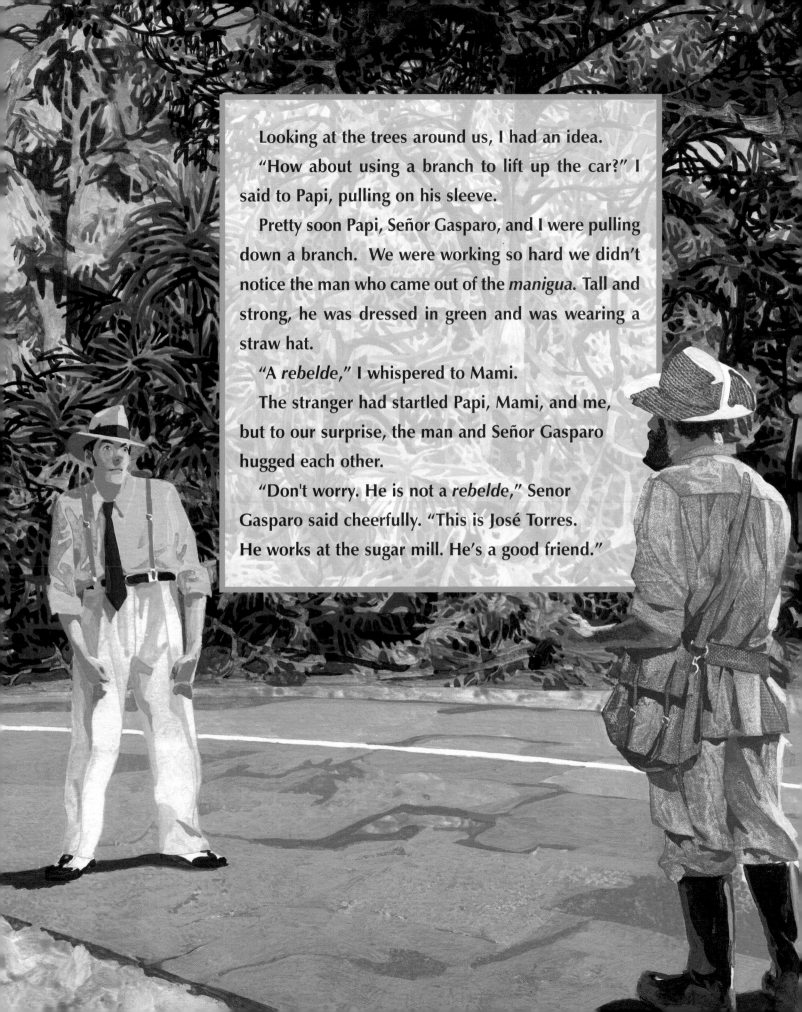

Looking at the trees around us, I had an idea.

"How about using a branch to lift up the car?" I said to Papi, pulling on his sleeve.

Pretty soon Papi, Señor Gasparo, and I were pulling down a branch. We were working so hard we didn't notice the man who came out of the *manigua*. Tall and strong, he was dressed in green and was wearing a straw hat.

"A *rebelde*," I whispered to Mami.

The stranger had startled Papi, Mami, and me, but to our surprise, the man and Señor Gasparo hugged each other.

"Don't worry. He is not a *rebelde*," Senor Gasparo said cheerfully. "This is José Torres. He works at the sugar mill. He's a good friend."

Señor Torres agreed to help us. He and Papi lifted the car while Señor Gasparo removed the flat tire and then put on the new one.

"There," Señor Gasparo said. "That didn't take too long."

Papi gave Señor Torres one of the bottles of *sidra* to thank him. As we drove off down the highway, we shouted, *"Feliz Navidad."* Merry Christmas.

The highway curved around the middle of the mountain, and on the other side was the town where we hoped to catch the bus to Santiago. Papi looked straight ahead, searching for the bus. A few minutes later, he spotted it on the horizon.

Señor Gasparo sped up. Little by little, he caught up with the bus. Inch by inch, he got in front of it.

Iiiiccchhh! the car screeched as Señor Gasparo braked to a full stop.

Iiiiccchhh! was the noise the bus made when it stopped a few feet away from the car.

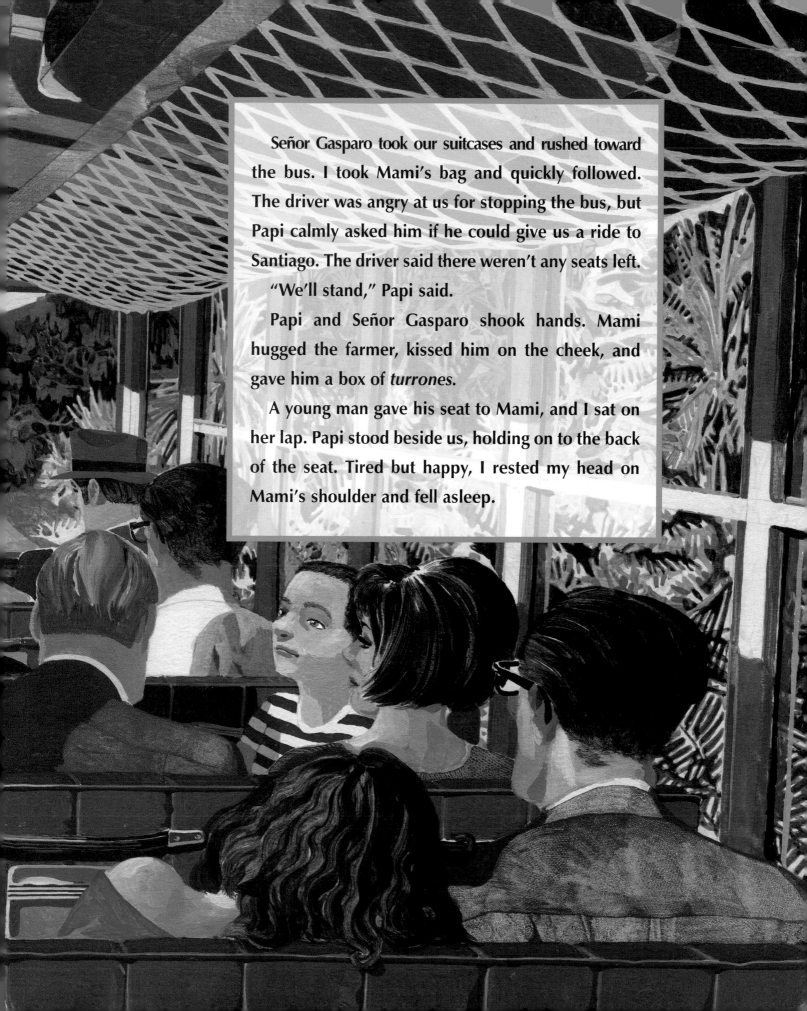

Señor Gasparo took our suitcases and rushed toward the bus. I took Mami's bag and quickly followed. The driver was angry at us for stopping the bus, but Papi calmly asked him if he could give us a ride to Santiago. The driver said there weren't any seats left.

"We'll stand," Papi said.

Papi and Señor Gasparo shook hands. Mami hugged the farmer, kissed him on the cheek, and gave him a box of *turrones*.

A young man gave his seat to Mami, and I sat on her lap. Papi stood beside us, holding on to the back of the seat. Tired but happy, I rested my head on Mami's shoulder and fell asleep.

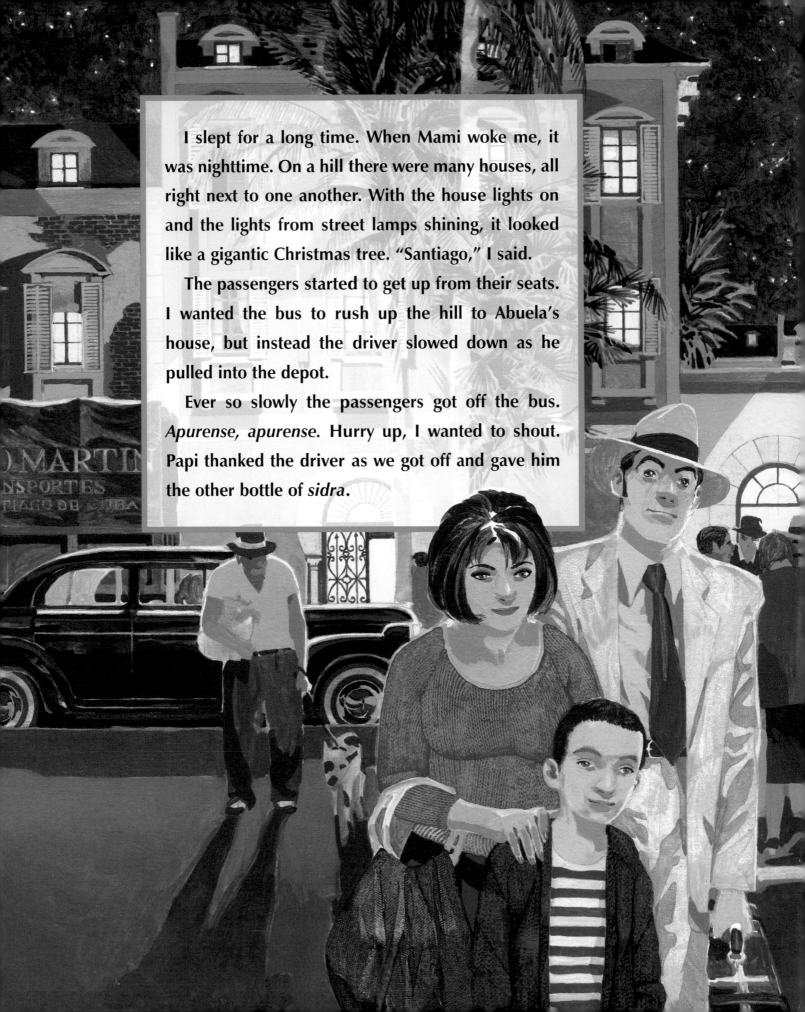

I slept for a long time. When Mami woke me, it was nighttime. On a hill there were many houses, all right next to one another. With the house lights on and the lights from street lamps shining, it looked like a gigantic Christmas tree. "Santiago," I said.

The passengers started to get up from their seats. I wanted the bus to rush up the hill to Abuela's house, but instead the driver slowed down as he pulled into the depot.

Ever so slowly the passengers got off the bus. *Apurense, apurense.* Hurry up, I wanted to shout. Papi thanked the driver as we got off and gave him the other bottle of *sidra*.

We quickly found a taxi and made our way to Abuela's house. It was on the corner, with many windows and a wide door. Music from the record player and sounds of laughter and merry voices spilled out of the house.

Mami, Papi, and I looked in from the doorway. There was the Christmas tree, just like always. And there was the long table that ran from the living room into the dining room. The dishes and silverware were on the table, but there was no food anywhere, even though the scent of roasted pork, boiled rice, beans, yucca, and fried plantains floated out from the kitchen. It was very late. Why weren't they eating?

My cousins were playing tag outside. My uncles were playing dominoes. My aunts were in the kitchen with Abuela.

"I'm starving," one of my uncles cried out. "I'm going to die if I don't eat soon!" Everybody laughed.

Abuela walked into the dining room. "We're not eating until we're all together," she said. "It doesn't matter how long . . ."

Just then Abuela saw us at the door, and a great big smile broke out on her face. She opened her arms wide and called out my name, "Alfredito." I ran toward her as Mami and Papi sang out, *"Feliz Navidad."*

All heads turned. My uncles scurried from the table as my aunts streamed in from the kitchen and my cousins rushed in from the courtyard. There were hugs and kisses all around. Several conversations went on at once as everyone asked about the war and the train and the *rebeldes*.

Papi tried to answer all the questions. Mami told them about the bus. I told my cousins about Señor Gasparo and Señor Torres.

"*Silencio!*" Abuela suddenly hushed everyone. The cathedral bells were tolling, beckoning all to *la misa del gallo.*

"We'll eat after mass," Abuela said. "We have a lot to be thankful for this year." She looked at all of us.

Most of the children wanted to stay home and eat, but we knew that Abuela always said what was right. So after allowing everyone to have a little snack, she watched us file out of the house.

Before I stepped out, Abuela held me back and handed me a paper bag.

The bag was warm. I opened it. Inside was a *buñuelo*, big and fat and dripping with honey!

"Feliz Navidad," Abuela said, and gave me another big hug.

I chewed the *buñuelo* slowly, savoring the sweet taste of the honey. The cathedral bells rang loudly, singing out to everyone that despite the war, it was still Christmas, it was still *Noche Buena,* and the world was still good and beautiful.